Piano • Vocal • Guitar

SONGS OF
ROMANCE

ISBN 0-7935-0025-7

This publication is not for sale in
the EC and/or Australia
or New Zealand

HAL•LEONARD®
CORPORATION
7777 W. BLUEMOUND RD. P.O. BOX 13819 MILWAUKEE, WI 53213

ALL I ASK OF YOU
(From "Phantom Of The Opera")

Music by ANDREW LLOYD WEBBER
Lyrics by CHARLES HART
Additional Lyrics by RICHARD STILGOE

ALL THE THINGS YOU ARE
(From "VERY WARM FOR MAY")

Words by OSCAR HAMMERSTEIN II
Music by JEROME KERN

trem - bles on the brink of a love - ly song.

You are the an - gel glow____ that light a

star,_____ The dear - est things I know____

____ are what you are._____

AND I LOVE HER

Words and Music by JOHN LENNON
and PAUL McCARTNEY

CAN'T HELP FALLING IN LOVE

Words and Music by
GEORGE DAVID WEISS, HUGO PERETTI,
and LUIGI CREATORE

Moderately Slow

CAN'T SMILE WITHOUT YOU

Words and Music by CHRIS ARNOLD,
DAVID MARTIN and GEOFF MORROW

THE COLOUR OF LOVE

Words and Music by WAYNE BRATHWAITE,
BARRY J. EASTMOND, BILLY OCEAN and JOLYON SKINNER

Cm7   **Eb/F**

see I've al - ways loved you right from the ver - y start.___ Tell me,{
like to take___ a look___ at e - mo - tions that you hide.___ Tell me,{

Bb   **Dm7**   **Cm**   **Eb/F**

What is the col - our of love?___ What do you see?___

Gm   **Dm7**   **Cm**   **Eb/F**

___ Is it warm,_____ is it ten - der_____ when you think of me?

COULD I HAVE THIS DANCE

Words and Music by WAYLAND HOLYFIELD
and BOB HOUSE

Moderately Slow

I'll al - ways re - mem - ber the song they were play - ing the
al - ways re - mem - ber that mag - ic mo - ment, when

first time_____ we danced and I knew.
I held_____ you close to me.
As we
As

DON'T KNOW MUCH

Words and Music by BARRY MANN,
CYNTHIA WEIL and TOM SNOW

ENDLESS LOVE

Words and Music by
LIONEL RICHIE

FOR ALL WE KNOW
(From The Motion Picture "LOVERS AND OTHER STRANGERS")

Words by ROBB WILSON and JAMES GRIFFIN
Music by FRED KARLIN

Moderato, with a light beat

MCA MUSIC PUBLISHING

FOREVER AND EVER, AMEN

Words and Music by DON SCHLITZ
and PAUL OVERSTREET

Lively Country

You may think that I'm_____ talk-in' fool-ish,
time takes that its on a bod-y,

heard that I'm wild_____ and I'm free._____
young gi-rl's brown_____ hair_____ turn gray.

makes you've
toll_____ makes a

HOW DEEP IS YOUR LOVE

Words and Music by BARRY GIBB,
MAURICE GIBB and ROBIN GIBB

Moderately

HERE AND NOW

Words and Music by TERRY STEELE
and DAVID ELLIOT

HOPELESSLY DEVOTED TO YOU

Words and Music by
JOHN FARRAR

HOW AM I SUPPOSED TO LIVE WITHOUT YOU

Words and Music by MICHAEL BOLTON
and DOUG JAMES

Verse 1:
I could hard-ly be-lieve it when I heard the news to-day. I had to come and get it straight from you.

Verse 2:
I'm too proud for cry-ing, did-n't come here to break down. It's just a dream of mine is com-in' to an end.

They said you are leav-in' some-one's
And how can I blame you when I

I'LL BE LOVING YOU (FOREVER)

Words and Music by
MAURICE STARR

IF I LOVED YOU
(From "CAROUSEL")

Words by OSCAR HAMMERSTEIN II
Music by RICHARD RODGERS

I.O.U.

Words and Music by AUSTIN ROBERTS
and KERRY CHATER

Moderately Slow Ballad

You be - lieve that I've changed your life _ for-ev - er _ and you're

- mazed when you say its me _ you live _ for _ and you

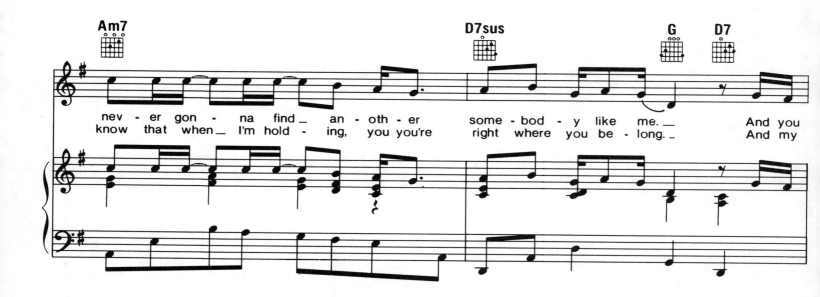

nev - er gon - na find _ an - oth - er some - bod - y like me. _ And you

know that when _ I'm hold - ing, you you're right where you be - long. _ And my

JUST THE WAY YOU ARE

Words and Music by
BILLY JOEL

JUST ONCE

Words by CYNTHIA WEIL
Music by BARRY MANN

LOST IN YOUR EYES

Words and Music by
DEBORAH GIBSON

LOVE ME TENDER

Words and Music by ELVIS PRESLEY
and VERA MATSON

Moderately slow

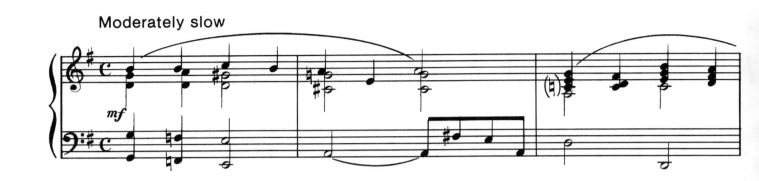

Verse

1. Love Me Ten - der, love me sweet;
2. Love Me Ten - der, love me long;
3. Love Me Ten - der, love me dear;

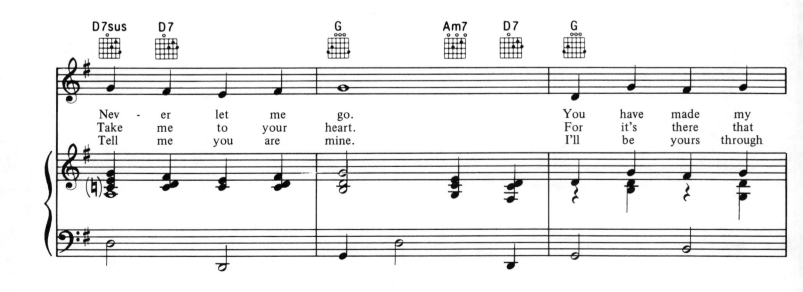

Nev - er let me go.
Take me to your heart.
Tell me you are mine.

You have made my
For it's there that
I'll be yours through

EXTRA VERSE   4. When at last my dreams come true,
Darling, this I know:
Happiness will follow you
Everywhere you go.

LONGER

Words and Music by
DAN FOGELBERG

Long - er than__ there've been fish - es in the o - cean,
Strong - er than__ an - y moun - tain cath e - dral.
Through the years__ as the fi - re starts to mel - low,

I'll_____ bring fi - re in__ the win - ters;___

you'll_____ send show-ers in__ the springs._____

We'll_____ fly through the falls and sum-mers with

love_____ on our__ wings.

MISTY

Words by JOHNNY BURKE
Music by ERROLL GARNER

MY FUNNY VALENTINE
(From "BABES IN ARMS")

Words by LORENZ HART
Music by RICHARD RODGERS

Slowly

My fun-ny Val-en-tine, Sweet com-ic Val-en-tine,

You make me smile with my heart.

Your looks are laugh-a-ble, Un-pho-to-graph-a-ble,

Yet, you're my fav-'rite work of art. _____ Is your

MY ROMANCE
(From "JUMBO")

Words by LORENZ HART
Music by RICHARD RODGERS

MORE
(Theme From MONDO CANE)

English Words by NORMAN NEWELL
Music by RIZ ORTOLANI and NINO OLIVIERO

Moderately

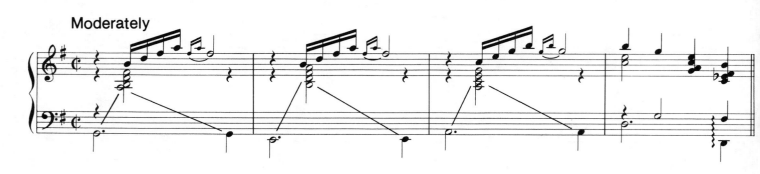

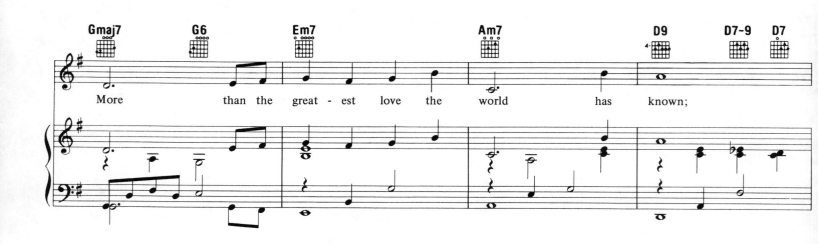

More than the great-est love the world has known;

This is the love I'll give to you a - lone.

SOMETIMES WHEN WE TOUCH

Words by DAN HILL
Music by BARRY MANN

OUR DAY WILL COME

Words by BOB HILLIARD
Music by MORT GARSON

Slowly, with expression

SOMEWHERE OUT THERE
(From "AN AMERICAN TAIL")

By JAMES HORNER,
BARRY MANN and CYNTHIA WEIL

Lyrics:

Some - where _____ out there be - neath the pale moon - light _____ some - one's think - in' of me and

MCA MUSIC PUBLISHING

through, then we'll be to-geth - er some-where out there, out

where dreams come true.

STRANGERS IN THE NIGHT

Words by CHARLES SINGLETON and EDDIE SNYDER
Music by BERT KAEMPFERT

Moderately slow

TRUE LOVE

Words and Music by
COLE PORTER

Moderately Slow

WHEN I FALL IN LOVE

Words by EDWARD HEYMAN
Music by VICTOR YOUNG

YOU DECORATED MY LIFE

Words and Music by DEBBIE HUPP
and BOB MORRISON

YOU NEEDED ME

Words and Music by
RANDY GOODRUM